THIS WALKER BOOK BELONGS TO:

_____

_____

_____

_____

For my granddaughter Isobel
P.L.

For Francesco
A.G.

First published 1994
by Walker Books Ltd, 87 Vauxhall Walk
London SE11 5HJ

This edition published 1996

2 4 6 8 10 9 7 5 3 1

This book has been typeset in Monotype Garamond.

Printed in Hong Kong

British Library Cataloguing in Publication Data
A catalogue record for this book is
available from the British Library.

ISBN 0-7445-4376-2

Good Night, Sleep Tight

Written by
Penelope Lively

Illustrated by
Adriano Gon

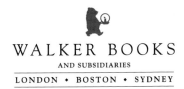

WALKER BOOKS
AND SUBSIDIARIES
LONDON • BOSTON • SYDNEY

There was once a girl who had a large family.

All day long she looked
after everybody.
She was rushed off her feet.

She washed and
shopped and cooked.

She read stories
and played games.

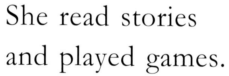

Sometimes
she got cross.

Other times she said she was worn to a frazzle and she must have a few minutes peace and quiet.

And at the end of the day she washed their faces

and cleaned their teeth and brushed their hair.

She read them a last story and then took them off to bed.

"Good night," said the girl. "Sleep tight."
And they all settled down to sleep.

"Who's kicking?" said the girl. "Who's
whispering? Who's jiggling about?"
Lion said, "We've got an idea."
The girl said, "We go to sleep now.
We don't have ideas."
Frog said, "We want to take you for
adventures. One adventure for each of us."
"I shall have to think about this," said the girl.
"Please," they all said. "Please."

So the girl said that if they promised to go straight off to sleep afterwards they could each of them take her for an adventure.

"Me first," said Frog. "I'm going to take you to the place where I live."

"You live here," said the girl. "In my house."

"Sometimes I do, and sometimes I don't. Sometimes I live at the bottom of the pond. The pond is where I do frog things," said Frog. "You can do them with me."

"I do deep diving.
I do fast swimming.
I do enormous jumping."

"More!" said the girl. "Again!"

"That's all for now," said Frog.
"It's someone else's turn."
    And they swam up out of the pond
    and *plop!* back into bed again.

"I go to a far away place," said Lion.
    "Only I know where it is.

I roar and I shout and I sing. You can join in. Nobody says stop making such a noise because there's nobody there."

They howled and they squealed and
they screamed. They made such a racket
that the ground shivered and
the stars shook.

"Louder!" shouted the girl.
They shrieked until
the leaves whirled and
the trees fell down.

"That'll do," said Lion.
"Let's have hush now."
 And back to bed they went.

"I go walking in the night," said Cat.
"Come on…"

"I go into the dark world
and I see things. I'm not afraid."
"Am I afraid?" asked the girl.
"No. You can see things too.
The world is huge and dark and
exciting. We go hunting
for surprises."
"Oooh…!" said the girl.
"Aaah…! What's that?"

"That's enough surprises," said Cat.
And they came out of the dark and into
the warm bed again.

"Me now," said Mary-Ann. "Hurry up!
We're going to the party."
"I haven't got a party dress," said the girl.
"Yes, you have," said Mary-Ann. "Look!
And here are all my friends.
Now they're your friends too."

"I don't know how to dance like that," said the girl.
"Yes, you do. Try. That's it… One, two, three. One, two, three."

And they danced and danced. They danced till they dropped, and then the girl said, "My feet hurt and I'm sleepy."

"Time to go home," said Mary-Ann.
"I'm too tired to walk," said the girl.
"You don't have to," said Mary-Ann,
"look where we are!"

And the girl looked,
and there she was
in her own bed.
And there beside her
were Frog and Lion
and Cat and Mary-Ann.
"Right," said the girl.
"Everybody settle down now.
We've had the adventures, and
it's time to sleep. Good night, sleep tight."
"Good night," they said.
"And if you're very good," said the girl,
"if you're very good and go straight to sleep,
and if you're good all day tomorrow,
we just might do it again one night."

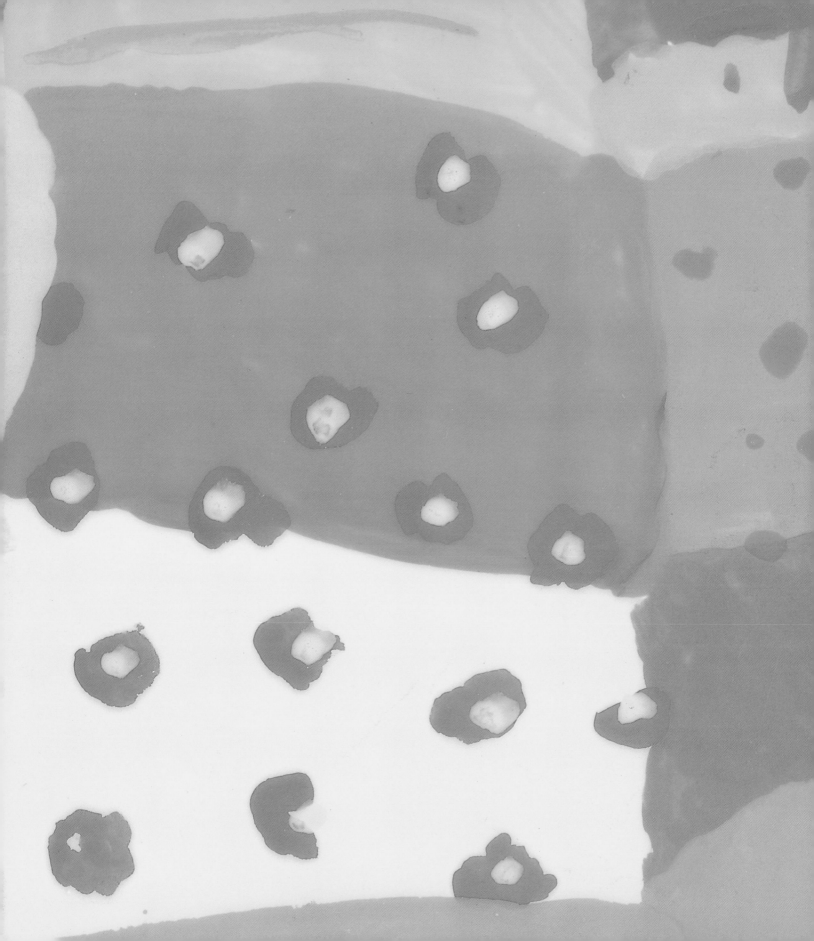

MORE WALKER PAPERBACKS
For You to Enjoy

THE CAT, THE CROW AND THE BANYAN TREE
by Penelope Lively/Terry Milne

All day long, the cat and the crow tell stories.
The cat's are elegant and entertaining; the crow's
are fast and furious. Each leads into the magical banyan tree.

"Imaginative and exciting… A classic storybook.
Terry Milne's illustrations are exquisite." *Baby*

0-7445-3633-2   £4.50

FINISH THE STORY, DAD
by Nicola Smee

"Humorously moral, *Finish the Story, Dad* tells of the amazing adventures
that Ruby gets sucked into all because her dad refuses to finish the story…
Nicola Smee tells a neat story." *Children's Books of the Year*

0-7445-3038-5   £3.99

THE WISH FACTORY
by Chris Riddell

Oliver used to have a bad dream about a monster, then one night
a cloud comes and takes him away to the wish factory…

"This glorious picture book, with its fantastic, highly imaginative illustrations,
has a special purpose: to drive away big bad dreams." *Practical Parenting*

0-7445-2328-1   £3.99

Walker Paperbacks are available from most booksellers, or by post from B.B.C.S., P.O. Box 941, Hull, North Humberside HU1 3YQ
24 hour telephone credit card line 01482 224626

To order, send: Title, author, ISBN number and price for each book ordered, your full name and address,
cheque or postal order payable to BBCS for the total amount and allow the following for postage and packing:
UK and BFPO: £1.00 for the first book, and 50p for each additional book to a maximum of £3.50.
Overseas and Eire: £2.00 for the first book, £1.00 for the second and 50p for each additional book.

Prices and availability are subject to change without notice.